TO

MW00909679

ANIMAL MAGIC

Written by

Alicia Love

Illustrated by

Kelly Lincoln

Paint Horse Publications ©2015
All Rights Reserved

*For Tom ~
Merry Christmas 2019
many Blessings,
Alicia*

CONTENTS

ACKNOWLEDGEMENTS

I would like to thank my dear friends and helpers whose time and talents contributed so much to the publishing of these stories.

Kelly Lincoln

Deborah and Stanley Marcus

Cady "Lucky' Fontana

Angela Walker

Erin Smith

Dr. Soundartus

And, of course, all of my animal friends

Thank you all so much!

Alicia Love

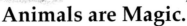

FOREWORD

Animals are Magic.

We are so accustomed to having them around, we

sometimes forget who they really are!

Here are some true animal adventures from my

life on Five Foxes Farm, where I welcome and

serve guests at the beautiful

Amazing Grace Bed and Breakfast.

Here, Animal Magic is a way of Life and a way of

Love. I am delighted to share these stories with

you and hope you will be inspired to create your

own Animal Magic wherever you are and

wherever you go.

- Alicia Love

FIN THE
RESCUE FISH

Fish make wonderful pets. No fur to vacuum, no enormous vet bills, no "accidents" on the carpets and no cold, soggy walks out into horrible weather. Ideal!

And while it's true they are rather lackluster in the cuddle department, they can, in fact, be very entertaining and even interactive. Fish are low maintenance, low impact and low budget. Lets take FIN the Rescue Fish for example. He cost $0.13 plus about $2.50 in food costs over the course of two years. Then, OK, there is the cost of housing. For just two dollars, I purchased the classic round glass fish bowl from our downtown

Salvation Army. Once home, I filled it with water, added a few pebbles and seashells, plus a spring of philodendron to aerate and purify the water. Lovely! And the total cost was less than $5.00. Now that's what I call affordable!

True enough, most fish are a wee bit more costly...but I bought Fin from the "Feeder Fish" tank. These are the fish slated to be something else's supper. There are billions of them, all crammed into a mid-sized tank...mainly smaller goldfish varieties. But if you are on a serious budget, and not particularly picky, a Feeder Fish is the way to go.

I bought Fin about four years ago after my son had adopted my former rescue fish, Spot, and his scaly pal, Blue. Now Blue was one of those stunningly beautiful $3.50 Fighter Fish. This species is fancy, with extravagant fins and lengthy tails, and very colorful, thus his name. Blue the Fighter Fish and Spot the Feeder Fish, against all odds, were on good terms, especially once they moved into the ten-gallon tank my son supplied for them soon after the adoption.

This was a real step up from the half-gallon fish bowl they had shared while youngsters, living with me! Fish adoption was one of my son's more successful attempts to stave off the Winter Blues. Where we live it can be overcast and cold for months at a time, and winter can last for half the year. Something to nurture and care for on a daily basis seemed to help a lot. My son was enjoying his fish so much, and my fish were enjoying their new tank so much, that I decided it was time to get another Rescue Fish.... for me! Just one. And he would have the whole bowl to himself!

It took awhile before I dared venture into the pet store. I often have a hard time buying only what I came in for. Pet stores are full of temptations for Pet Lovers like me. I waited until I had a friend to go in with, and I explained my mission.

We did manage to look at everything in the store with fur or feather, reminiscing over former guinea pigs, white rats and parakeets, and exploring the option of finding another orange-colored canary like Mango, the one I had years ago. But, fortunately for me, my friend was on a schedule and kept me on track. She reminded me of the time, and then we moved toward the Fish Department. I quickly glanced over tank after tank filled with fancy guppies, mollies and high-dollar fish, before I finally stopped at my destination: the $0.13 Feeder Fish tank.

It was lively with a bazillion small orange fish darting frantically to and fro. They must have just gotten a new shipment! This is the tank where the clients generally bought in bulk, having little attachment to the stylish looks or personality of their purchase. I was the rare, one-item-only Feeder Fish client. I stared at the perpetual motion before me and began to search for My Fish...

This is how I remember it...out of the masses of scaly golden bodies, up swam one small majoritively white fish with a golden crown and cape. He stared at me, swimming back and forth and back and forth.

It was like he *knew* he was My Fish! But, it may have been different. It may have been overwhelming trying to figure out which one of these many, many teeny-weeny, itty-bitty, fishy-wishies was going be the lucky new resident of my $2.00 fishbowl. I was looking for a fish of distinction, and this little guy certainly fit the bill. But either way, I was hooked! I called over the gal with the little fish net and pointed him out.

Patiently and kindly she took the time to swoop up exactly the right fish from among the throngs. She plopped him into a little plastic sack with some water in it, and away I went to the check-out counter. Oops! Forgot the fish food! So back I went, picked out the smallest possible container, then plunked down the BEST $3.00 I've ever spent.

Once home, I had fun setting up his new residence. I still had the pebbles and plenty of plant clippings, so in a matter of minutes, his home was complete. I waited an hour for the water temperature to equalize. Then I dumped him gently from the plastic sack into his new home, and he became the official King of the Fish Bowl. He was so excited! Back and forth and back and forth and round and round he went. He seemed as excited for his new home as I was for my new fish. I placed his bowl on the entrance table by my door.

I named him "FIN: KING OF THE FISH BOWL", but I called him just "Fin" for short. Now, when I first brought Fin home, he was only little. Of course, I loved him and he was beautiful ... to me! But really, he was rather ordinary in many ways. I think, however, his location by the entrance to my home has been one of the determining factors in this small creature's destiny. Because he is right there to wave goodbye to me on the way out, and to greet me upon return, he is an ever-present personality.

Every morning, I stop to feed him when going out to tend to the horses and the chickens. He soon began to swim over to greet me each morning, swimming back and forth, back and forth and waving his little fins, as if to say, "Hi Big Person! Hi! See Me? See Me? Don't forget ME!!" Ha! Ha! Cute little guy!

Of course, I don't forget Fin...and I give him three to five tiny pellets for breakfast, which certainly makes his trip across the bowl worth his efforts. If he hasn't quite noticed me, I tap gently on the side of his glass bowl. Now, whenever I tap his bowl, he swims on over for a little interaction! I wave back at Fin, wiggling my fingers. I believe he thinks these are his friends. Fin will even eat from my fingertip! I keep his food in a small porcelain swan, originally designed as a salt cellar. I ever so slightly moisten my finger, then I gently touch his food, so that only a few grains of it will stick.

Then ...tap tap tap... over Fin swims and I carefully place my finger just above his head near the surface of the water. Fin pokes his little fishy face out of the water and chomps the tiny food pallet off my fingertip. I can just feel the touch of his tiny fishy lips for a second, but it is a thrill. It is rather astonishing to experience such a strong bond with a cold-blooded little animal, with gills and scales, living in water! In almost every way, he is different from me! Yet, it is a bond of Joy and Trust, and true Affection. There is no question in my mind that all living things have emotions of sorts...and all respond to Love.

Another, perhaps unscientific, but surely amazing observations about Fin: King of the Fish Bowl, is how he came to live into his name. Perhaps it is really only a matter of genetics... but Fin was just an ordinary little fish when I bought him, with ordinary little fins.

Today, he is large and lovely. His fins and tail are long and luxurious, with an opaque quality to them that seems almost magical. In his bowl, the philodendron sprigs have sent down long thick roots which grow amid the castle I gave him for Christmas last year. He swims majestically through his green underwater palace arrayed in his regal attire, looking every bit as beautiful as any high-dollar fish will ever look. Perhaps, it is just MY perception of Fin, looking at him through the Lens of Love. Or perhaps, just perhaps, it is LOVE that works its Magic and changes all it touches from the Common...and the Royal.

HOPPING HEN HENNA

By the time Henna had come to live in the henhouse here at Amazing Grace Bed and Breakfast, I had long ago stopped giving names to my chickens. "Naming" was something for first time hen owners and children; by then, I was neither. I had kept chickens for 20 years, wanting to serve only the best farm fresh eggs to my family and guests. But in that time, I had lost so many of my flock to the wild creatures (foxes, hawks, coyotes, skunks, raccoons and even mink!) that I had abandoned the practice of personalizing each bird. It somehow made the losses a bit easier. However, every now and then, every few years or so, there would come along a hen well deserving of a name. And such a one was Hopping Hen Henna.

I cannot recall exactly how Henna came to live here. There are so many ways to gain hens! Often, especially when my children were young, we would purchase our chickens through a mail-order catalog. We always did this with one other family who also raised chickens and had children the same ages as mine.

The hatcheries needed to send out at least twenty chicks with each order - the chicks kept each other warm during shipping. Neither one of our families needed twenty new hens each year, so we always placed our order together. Kathy and I would spend hours on the phone and loved pouring over the pages of the Chicken Catalogs! There are so many different breeds, different sizes, shapes and colors. Each breed lays its own color and not just white or brown! Some varieties lay pink, blue, and even green eggs! It was always hard to choose which breeds to purchase, but each of our families would end up ordering about eight to twelve hens, of three different varieties. A few weeks later, we would make an early morning trip to the post office to pick up a peeping box of day-old chicks.

It was always an exciting time! This mission was often accompanied by a day off from school for our children, so we could all enjoy each other and settle our baby birds into their new homes. The kids would take turns choosing chicks for each family's henhouse, placing each family's chicks in a separate cardboard box. This process would often take over an hour, while the children debated over which ball of fluff would go with them. Of course, Kathy and I would be sure the children knew which varieties each family had ordered. Then when all was settled, we'd take a break for breakfast.

But our work was not done! The babies needed special attention, of course, as they had no other mother but us to tend to them. So after our meal, my family would take our chicks straight home. We would spend the rest of the morning preparing a "Chick-box". Ours was a large galvanized tub, with a wire mesh "roof", lined with newspaper or brown paper bags, then fluffed up with wood shavings.

We'd add to that a heat lamp, a water dispenser and some "chick-start" (baby-food for chickens), and their new home was complete. The Chick-box needed to stay inside the house for the first few weeks, so that we could keep an eye on our new brood, making sure they stayed warm, dry, healthy and safe from predators. As a result, we all spent a fair amount of time with the new baby chicks. Since each breed has unique markings, even as little ones, those fluff balls provided hours upon hours of entertainment for us all. Their appearance and personalities, and our imaginations, inspired special chick-names, like Peepster, Chippie, and Sunflower. Inevitably there were some losses and sorrows, as all baby animals are fragile, but most of our chicks grew quickly, and were healthy and strong. By late Spring, they were ready for the great outdoors. By late Fall they would be laying eggs!

Another way we occasionally expanded our flock was simply to barter or purchase full grown hens from someone else's flock.

And while this was not nearly as much fun, neither was it as much work, and this method had the additional value of allowing us to get hens who were already laying eggs. This way of obtaining hens occurred mainly in mid-summer, after some horrible and heinous henhouse invasion by some chicken-eating wildlife! Foxes were particularly sneaky.

Once they had eaten a chicken dinner, you could be sure they would come back for more....and more ....and MORE!!!! Most often they would make their first raid at night, while the hens were asleep!

Once even one hen is lost to a fox, EVERYTHING changes. Day and night the hens would disappear. Naturally, I would be more diligent in locking the henhouse door exactly at sunset, when they came in to roost. But that was not enough! The fox wanted more chicken and was determined to get it! He would lurk on the edge of the pasture or in the woods, waiting for me to let the hens out in the morning. If I spied him, I would chase him back into the woods! But, oh that wily Fox! He would stop his retreat as soon as I had turned around, and come sneaking back behind me!

I had learned that lesson the hard way, losing a hen just minutes after I had returned to my house, confident I had chased the fox away...and I have caught him at this practice at least twice after that! And so this meant I had to stand guard even during the day, protecting the flock. Well, finally I bought a gun! I would teach that fox a lesson! It is interesting, however, how much the wildlife actually teach us. One Honest Fox taught me a lesson, and that is quite an amazing story...... but I will tell that one to you later.

Now, Mr. Fox was not the only wild animal that loved to eat my Chickens. Mink, Skunk, Weasels, and Coyotes sometimes got them, too. But the WORST offenders of all were the Raccoons! They are extremely smart and would figure out clever ways to open the henhouse door! Then, they would throw a big party and invite their friends to the hen house. They would take bites out of each and every bird and scatter the remains of hens everywhere, never bothering to clean up after themselves. It was horrible! I hated to go to the hen house after raccoons had been there.

As a result of these various traumatic tragedies, I spent many an hour mending fences, putting up electric wiring and chasing foxes! After each new effort, I always believed the Henhouse was secure.

Come to think of it, it was after just such a massacre and fence mending binge that I went to my pal Kathy to see if she had an extra hen or two she could spare. My henhouse was quite sparse after the last wildlife raid...and it was summertime, the middle of my Bed and Breakfast season. I needed hens! I needed eggs! Kathy sent me home with some fine, fat gals that knew how to lay. And one of them was a darling, bright-eyed Rhode Island Red.

Now, Rhode Island Reds are an extremely common backyard breed. But this little Rhodie had a special personality. She was overtly friendly and playfully affectionate. Why, she would actually run to greet me whenever I came outside. True enough, I took table scraps out to the chickens almost daily, feeding them on cracked corn in the fine weather, and warmed corn meal or soup on the frozen mornings in the winter months. Still, none of the other gals ever expressed their appreciation quite as exuberantly as she did. Her antics were so endearing, it was impossible not to take notice of her. Before long, I was looking forward to seeing her as much as she was looking forward to seeing me. I christened her "Henna", the perfect name for a little red hen!

Back then we also had two horses on the farm. Growing in the yard were three generously bearing apple trees: a red, a green, and a golden variety. The green "Granny Smiths" were the nearest in proximity to the animals. Every morning, as the days grew shorter and colder, on my way out to feed the animals, I'd pick three apples: two for the horses, and one for the hens and me.

I'd start my every day with a few tasty bites of those flavorful, juicy apples. Then, when I was getting near the henhouse, I'd chomp off a big bite and chew it up just a little, enough so the apple was in little warm bits for the hens. Upon arrival, I'd let the chickens out, then spit the apple bits, watermelon seed style, all over the hen yard. They would dive in—a feeding frenzy! Oh how they loved their warm apple breakfast!

One crisp Autumn morning, standing in the hen yard, chomping on an apple and conversing with my feathered friends, I was astonished to find the apple no longer in my hand... What on earth??

Picking the fruit back up and brushing it off on my leg, I noticed Henna jumping off the ground and all aflutter to get another bite! It was she who had knocked the apple from my hand! Ha! That silly little hen just couldn't get enough! Up she popped again! Peck! And then again! Peck! I was completely astonished and amused. Watching with delight, I held the apple higher and higher...and each time she just hopped higher and higher to get another bite. What a funny little character she was!

The next morning, I was out again with an apple. Would Henna repeat her performance of yesterday? I opened the hen-house door, and when all the chickens were out I did my usual warmed-up applebits distribution. Henna, along with the others, pecked happily at the bits, but then, when they were gone, she tilted her golden head up at me. I held the apple up where she could plainly see it.

She fixed upon it with her beady eyes, then HOP! Up she sprang in a flutter of feathers! With amazing skill and accuracy, she pecked a bit of apple! Again and again, there was no stopping her! How I laughed and laughed at her adorable antics. She was hilarious! I just had to show a friend! So I called my friend Cassie and asked her to come by to see my performing poultry. I was curious to see if Henna would willingly perform in the company of others. Cassie, I thought, was the perfect candidate, someone Henna might be comfortable around. Cassie and I rode horses together. She was over quite a bit and had even, on occasion, watched my flock while I was out of town. Plus, she had chickens of her own AND she lived nearby. Cassie was curious.

She was over in minutes, on her way to work. I had also promised coffee! We grabbed a quick cup of Java, and then out to the hen yard we strode, plucking an apple on the way. Again, and without hesitation, Henna displayed her Hop-and-Peck skills. Cassie was just as amused as I was. We raised the apple higher and higher, till Henna was hopping a good 4 feet into the air. Thus began our new morning routine, with occasional Bed and Breakfast guests as an appreciative audience, until I was confident of her skills and dedication.

"Well!" thought I, "This little hen and I are about ready for the circus!.

"Ladies and Gentleman.... Introducing the World Famous Hopping Hen Henna!"

We had BIG plans for the Bigtop!

Well, we never made it to the circus, and Henna never quite became a world-famous Hen. But, she did become a popular sideshow here at Amazing Grace Bed and Breakfast. Henna would spy our small group tromping out to see her, and come running over, wobbling back and forth on her two scaly, yellow legs...always full of anticipation...and hop and hop...a full five feet for her apples! She performed for family and friends alike, here in the Ithaca area, and for my guests from around the world! She amused us all, young and old, who willingly ventured out to the barnyard to visit this exceptional little animal.

In all my years on the farm she was the sweetest and funniest hen I ever had. I loved that little bird, and Hopping Hen Henna will remain ever-famous in my heart!

POETRY - A Crow Story

Anyone can tell you: there are "good" birds...and then, thereare "bad" birds. Or, at least, that's what most people think. The "good" birds are the pretty, little colorful ones that sing lovely and melodious songs.... and the "BAD" birds, well, they are the Squawkers, the big black kind, the ones that eat dead things, like Buzzards! But worst of ALL, are the ones who eat the eggs and babies of the "Good Birds"! Right? Like CROWS! Right? Well...no. Not really.

All birds play an important role in the ecosystem, although there are some birds that we, as humans, perhaps enjoy more than others. But even the ones that we might think of as unattractive actually do good and necessary things! For instance, the big scary vultures that eat dead things are actually, really very useful.

They clean up after Nature! All things do eventually die, so it is good to have a few creatures that like to help tidy up. The vultures and crows do exactly that. And they enjoy it! After all, they are getting a free meal!

And, can you believe it? Many people don't even like Blue Jays. Although they are very beautiful and colorful birds, they are also loud, raucous squawkers, and notorious for thieving eggs. But they actually have a well-rounded vocabulary and can make a very lovely trill that sounds almost like water. And, they are very smart. They evaluate situations and respond accordingly. Most birds are completely wary of humans, but Jays and Crows will assess a person or situation as either advantageous or dangerous. I will never forget when high winds blew down a nest of baby Blue Jays from a pine tree growing right next to our house. The nestlings were fully feathered youngsters, just a few days away from fledging. They were just beginning to develop the trademark peaked crest on top of their heads, only they weren't quite there yet.

They looked ridiculous! Just like little Cone Heads. They were so cute and so funny that I spent a bit of time with them enjoying these awkward baby birds. I fed them some banana, then I scooped them up and gently placed them back into their nest. I then placed the nest in a safe location on the roof, under the boughs of the pine tree. The mother Jay had squawked and fussed, watching me intently while I rescued her brood. Maybe she was giving me instructions on how to proceed!! She must have approved, as I had the joy of watching that momma Jay accept the new location and teach those silly birdies to fly!

Crows, also, have definitely been given a bad reputation, which is reflected in movies and storybooks. Crows almost always play the Villain Bird or the Trickster Bird. Because of this, there have been three attempts to exterminate them here in America, killing thousands upon thousands of these amazing birds. But Crows, as recent university studies have shown, are literally some of the most intelligent animals on the planet. In fact they are very much like us.

For example, they build their nests in close proximity to one another, creating small Crow Cities. They help raise each other's babies, which they feed with a broad and varied diet. They even provide toys for their young! Plus, crows all have individual names for one another. They have an extensive vocabulary, and an advanced social structure. In fact, there is tribe of Native Americans who long ago took the name "Crow", to proudly proclaim their own intelligence. Crows will also warn each other and other birds when predators, especially Hawks, are searching for a meal. Some people think Crows are saying "Caw! Caw!"... but I imagine they are really saying, "Hawk! Hawk!", announcing the large predatory birds, giving the other crows, and all the woodland and meadowland creatures a chance to hide, escape, or prepare for warfare! Because of their intelligence, Crows have always held a certain fascination for me, and for many years I longed to have one to train.

Over the course of time, I had discovered some Crow nesting sites. But I didn't feel right stealing a baby bird from her Momma and nestlings.

However, my prayers were answered one fine May afternoon. I had opened the windows to air out the rooms of my Bed and Breakfast when I heard a huge ruckus down by the pond. The Red-winged Blackbirds nesting there were all in a dither.

"Hmmm", thought I. "Just yesterday Crow rokkery in the woods just beyond the pond, were in a huge uproar for hours! Now the Redwings right by the pond are in an uproar. Perhaps that raccoon, or hawk, or whatever it was that had been messing with the Crows, is down there now messing with the Redwings". I scurried outside to see what was going on. Down to the pond I ran, to where the Redwings had nested for twenty consecutive years in the tall cattails along the water's edge.

The Crows' rookery was way too high up in the pines and too deep in the wood for me to be able to defend them, but I could potentially help the Redwings. Maybe, it was yesterday's scoundrel, raiding more nests. I was curious to find out who and what it was. I was hoping this was not a case of feline mischief! My cats, having an ample supply of barn rodents and cat crunchies, did not tend to do much birding. Upon occasion however, I would see piles of feathers here and there. I was so hoping they had not gone after the Redwings!

But Lo and Behold! When I got to water's edge, I found no cat, raccoon or hawks! No Predators at all! Just a short, fat black baby bird. A fledgling Crow! A dream come true! It must have fallen out of the rookery in yesterday's scuffle. I was thrilled! I scooped up the frightened little thing and brought it up to the house. I gave it a fingerful of wet cat food, and instantly it became my best friend. For me, it was love at first sight. For the crow, it was love at first bite!

I named him "Poetry".

In his first few days with me, Poetry lived in a birdcage on the kitchen counter. I spent a lot of time in the kitchen, so that with him right there by me, we could get to know one another. Also, I could be right there to meet the demands of his voracious appetite!

When I found him, he could not yet fly. But he grew in amazing leaps and bounds. In just a couple of days, he had already outgrown that cage, so I put him outside in a huge former ferret cage under the pines, just outside the back door. Being a farm girl, I was up at first light, which is when Po began to cry for some breakfast. Then, after he ate, he would hop on my shoulder and I would do my chores...feeding the horses and the chickens, and working in the garden. He would just stay perched there, playing with my earrings and biting my hair, most of the day.

He soon began to flutter and show some interest in flying. I helped him with his flying lessons as best I could, scooping him up after a trial flight and holding him at a safe distance from the ground for future flight attempts. He was a brilliant student, soon flying from my shoulder to low branches. He gained a certain independence, but still stayed near my work areas. When I went into the house, he would go to the spruce just outside the door and wait for me.

His next big step came one day when I needed to leave the house before dusk, which is when he would always flutter down to me so I could tuck him in his cage for the night. It was too early for him to go to bed, and he had no interest in responding to my "Come-Po" plea, which he ordinarily had done. In fact, Po was rather making a game of it! He seemed to like me chasing and coaxing after him while he kept just slightly out of reach. Silly bird! I was nervous to leave him out of his cage for the night... so many predators, including my own cats, loved to eat baby birds!! But he simply would not come to me that day. I think it was his way of saying, "I'm too grown-up for my bird cage babysitter!" So. Away I drove, praying for his safety.

Thus began our new routine. Po was camped out in the Spruce when I got home late that night, and up and eagerly awaiting his breakfast in the morning. He seemed perfectly comfortable with the new, cage-less situation, and so it remained. For the next few months, he slept among the evergreens at night, and rode on my shoulder and followed me around with great interest during the day. He was so smart and watched me keenly. One day, on a special visit, my stepmom Sally was weeding in the garden, when Po fluttered off my shoulder and onto the ground. He then began to hop around in the soil, pulling the tiny new weeds from the garden. It suddenly occurred to Sally that Po was imitating her!! She ran over to tell me. What a fine little fellow he was! Helping us weed the garden! He was adorable!

It was also clear that he was learning from me, and I felt I must teach him some Crow survival skills. Rather than feed him in one location, as I had been doing, I began to put food scraps out in various places around the yard, so he could learn to actually look for his own food. He would need that skill once he was mature and back in the wild. I had no intention of caging him again and so he had to learn to do what birds do in order to survive!

I had also become aware that more and more Crows had begun to gather daily in the small copse beyond the horse pasture. It was almost impossible not to notice them, as they called incessantly. Clearly they had noticed that their long lost Baby Bird was actually alive and well and living in the Spruce! I watched with interest as the crows grew in number and flew a bit closer to the house each day. It seemed they wanted to get a closer look to see if this really could be their prodigal son!

The morning came when I went out with Po's breakfast, but he was not there. I was startled! I began to call all around for him. I wandered into the back yard, and there in the horse pasture was a large flock of crows all on the ground. I called for Po. All the birds flew away...except one. Po! He flew right to me! My Poetry! My sweet little Poetry! I was so relieved, so amazed, so happy!! !

Poetry spent the entire rest of that day with me, just doing what we always did. But the next morning he was not there, and I never saw him again.

I like to think his flock called him back and he met and married a very special Crow lady who happened to also be a great cook. But that was also the worst year for the West Nile Virus, so deadly to Crows. Crows are reliable visitors. Once a bond has been formed they always return to visit. But Po never visited me ever again.

I will never know what really happened to Po, but I like to think of him as happily married. Perhaps his wife is jealous that she can't offer Po the mashed bananas, cat food, and dinner scraps as good as "Mom" used to give him... or perhaps she is skeptical and un-trusting of humans, flatly refusing to let Po come visiting. Who can say? To this very day, whenever a crow flies near me, I call out for Poetry. Wherever he is, I do know he made one of my dearest dreams come true and I have been blessed to have gotten the chance to make friends with a very, very special Crow.

NASHVILLE AND NUGGET GO TRAVELING

Of all the curious and unexpected behaviors of the various animals I have befriended over the years, the most astonishing of all was one peculiar episode with Nashville and Nugget, Rooster and Hen. The accolades here must go almost entirely to Nugget, as Nashville was a reticent and sometimes annoying participant. The fact that he participated at all surely allows him at least partial credit. But really, it was Nugget's idea...which in itself is thought provoking.

What would ever possess a hen to want to go to a wedding? A wedding that requires a two-day drive in a cage to get there? How does a hen even know what a wedding is? This will always remain a great mystery to me... but nonetheless, it was clear Nugget wanted to

Now, for the last couple of years, I had been in a band. We called ourselves "The Coyote Cowgirls" and we played an amusing assortment of cowgirl and old-timey music, which occasionally involved some hens and goats ...for emphasis. We were a fun band! Sometimes in fine weather we'd play outside in the yard surrounded by farm animals large and small! And, once, we had even brought some chickens and our mischievous baby black goat, Liquor-ish, into the house to make a music video!

And as it happened while our Band played music in backyards and bars, festivals and cafes, Twy the Fiddle Player and John the Bouzouki Player fell in Love. After a while, John needed to move back to Indiana for his job. Well, by then Twy and John were engaged to be married... so they both moved to Indiana together to do all that. Of course, they invited me to the wedding... a three-day affair involving loads of Love, Food, and Fun, lots and lots of Music and a Coyote Cowgirl Show at a place called "The Cabin".

But first I had to get to Indiana, hundreds of miles away! I would be driving what had fondly become known as "The Cowgirl Truck", an old '89 Chevy pickup we had painted for a Parade some years before. We had also used it as a mobile stage for our band. It had a huge Peace Sign on the hood, and COYOTE COWGIRLS blazing in a variety of colors across the side. Along with numerous other embellishments, many of the letters on the tailgate had been painted over so that the originally embossed C-

H- E- V- R- O- L- E- T had become, instead, H- E-
R –O- E . It was a real piece of road art.

The day of my departure I was busily making my
traveling preparations, packing my instruments
and a suitcase, cleaning and loading the truck. I
backed down the driveway to the side entrance of
the house and popped out to get some supplies,
leaving the truck doors open for a little minute. In
the house I gathered together the glass cleaner,
rags and all, then headed back out to put a new
shine on the ol' Chevy.

Upon return, I was astonished to find my little
golden hen, Nugget, standing on the front seat of
the pickup and staring through the windshield.
Never, no never! had any chicken climbed aboard
any of my vehicles, so I wondered what on earth
had possessed Nugget to do so that day. I gently
lifted her out, admonishing her while stroking
her beautiful feathers.

"Silly little Hen! What are you thinking? Do you want to go to the Wedding? " Laughing at the thought of it, I placed her on the driveway and began my truck cleaning project.

Earlier in the week, I'd had the camper top put on so I could make a cozy arrangement for myself in the back of the truck. And cozy it was! It would take two days to drive to Bloomington, Indiana,and I much prefer to just rest in my vehicle for a couple hours here and there to hoteling it when I'm traveling. I furnished the camper with a narrow but comfy mattress piled high with flannel sheets, antique quilts and an array of cushy pillows.

I added my book and a flashlight, a window box filled with herbs, a five gallon bucketed cherry tomato plant, creating a "home away from home" effect. Then back into the house I went for a few more supplies. Oh, but then the phone rings, I make lunch, I reconsider my travel wardrobe, and in general get distracted. But finally, back out to the truck I go.

Ok! What's this? There I stood with an armload of instruments, staring at Nugget. She had fluttered and flapped her way up and into the camper. And there she stood, on my quilts! I was completely astonished, and certainly amused, to find the hen once again in the truck. I quickly shooed her out before I had hen-poop on my bedding!

But when she jumped out, instead of running off with Nashville to search for bugs, she just stayed right there by me near the back of the truck as I worked.

"What are you doing, Nugget?" I asked her. She gave no other reply than to stand there, head cocked, staring up at me with her beady eye. "What are you thinking, LITTLE HEN? Do you

REALLY want to go to the Wedding? 'Cuz, if you do, you are going to have to ride in a crate! You can't just run around free back here, pooping everywhere, ya know." I almost felt like I was talking more to myself than to her, yet while I loaded in the water jug, fruit and granola bars. Nugget made yet another attempt to express herself. Up she flapped into the truck bed AGAIN!

"OK then, Girl ! ", I said, chuckling, and went straight away to the henhouse. I got out the largest hen crate I had and filled it with hay. I found a perfect stick that sufficed as a roost, and filled a couple shallow custard bowls with cracked corn and water. She, like I, now had a portable home! I took it to the end of the driveway and placed it near the tailgate for her approval.

"Nugget," I said. "Here it is, your mobile home! If you REALLY want to come with me, I will bring you along! But you'll have to ride in your own little home."

She strode right on over and circled the crate twice, slowly, just checking out the whole arrangement. Then she stood outside the door, stretching her head way in, for a look around. I guess it passed muster, as she then ventured in, pecked some corn and settled down into the hay. I closed the door behind her, with Nugget exhibiting no visible signs of stress. I then placed the mini henhouse on a piece of black plastic inside the camper, next to the herbs. Little Nugget certainly knew how to pack light! She was ready to go!

"Well. Great! " I thought. "But what about Nashville? What is HE going to do? Is he going to want to stay home alone?" The ol' boy had exhibited none of the enthusiasm for travel that his companion did. Well, I wasn't going to force the issue.

It was already more than I had bargained for to travel with one chicken, let alone a cranky, crowing Rooster!

Still, I was nervous to leave him alone for five days! Nashville and Nugget were the only chickens I had left! Summer had begun with a good healthy flock of twelve. Now, I had but two. It all began with a disappearing hen act that a local fox den had been involved with. After that loss, for their protection, I had actually divested myself of some hens by giving a starter flock to my pal, Eric, and selling three others to some first time hen owners. Nashville, being a "Roo", was not in much demand, so he stayed here with me on the farm. He had actually been born in my hand, so I had a special fondness for him anyway. But chickens are flock animals and like companionship. So I kept Nugget as well. She was such a friendly girl, she had always been my favorite!

The two were like an old married couple so I was hoping Nashville would come along.

With that fox still on the loose, if he stayed home alone, I knew he might not be there when I got back!

My plan was for an afternoon departure. I only had about another hour of preparation before I'd be ready. It is near impossible to catch a loose rooster, and I had no intentions of spending my time running all over the yard trying to catch him, or waiting for hours 'til dark, when he'd go to the henhouse to roost. So, I just went about my business. Nashville would have to decide.

The ol' boy seemed to be aware that something was up. He and Nugget ordinarily strolled the grounds of the B&B together, hunting for tender bugs and tasty greens. Now here she was at midday, contentedly ensconced in a crate in the back of the pickup. Nugget was clearly determined to go, with or without Nashville, and she must have figured she had him over a barrel. Chickens are, after all, flock animals. They are not comfortable being alone. Since the diminishment of the flock, Nugget had been Nashville's singular and constant companion. Married life had been challenge enough for the old Roo, but bachelorhood was too much. Within the hour ol' Nashville had hopped into the camper, too. He went immediately over to Nugget and checked out the new digs. Fortunately I was in the camper too, and was able to slyly open the door of the crate.

Nashville, with the encouragement of Nugget, the corn and a small shove-in from me, was Indiana-bound!

In less than an hour, we were headed west. The poultry travelled surprisingly well, and Nugget, who seemed absolutely thrilled at the prospect of a vacation, laid an egg of visible contentment. For the fresh grass and exercise the chickens would enjoy at Rest Stops, I had brought long pieces of bailing twine and tied them onto dog leashes. Before letting the chickens out, I gently tied the bailing twine loosely but securely around one of their scaly legs. The twine was light enough to allow freedom of motion, but the dog leash was just heavy enough to slow them down. They could peck around freely for the length of the twine, but once past that point, they would feel a pull. It was ideal. By the time half the journey was behind us, clever little Nugget needed no leash at all! She would just hop back into the truck as soon as Nashville was in the cage. I was astonished! What an amazing little gal she was! The three of us in the Ol' Cowgirl Truck made quite the Rest Stop Spectacle, I'm sure !

Now, at this point, I must admit that no one at the Indiana Wedding, including the Bride and Groom, had any idea I was bringing these "additional guests". I had decided, after Nugget's last minute insistence upon coming, that perhaps this fine pair of poultry could make a wonderful wedding gift. So I left it a surprise.

So when we arrived, the greetings were warm and riotous. The Chicken addition was met with a delightful mix of astonishment and hilarity. And while both Twy and John were none to eager to actually adopt them, they were happy enough to host the Wedding Crashers temporarily. Naturally, both Nugget, and especially Nashville, were overjoyed to be at last let loose upon the nuptial grounds.

He burst from the confining cage, all a-flutter, and began to strut and preen and crow to the charm of the assembled party. Nugget casually ambled forth, fixed us all with her beady eye, then strolled about, scratching and pecking as if it were perfectly natural for her to have traveled hundreds of miles to hunt bugs in Indiana! They behaved exactly like chickens and we were all delighted and amused. They made themselves completely at home. Nugget scoped out the large evergreen tree near the front porch to be their evening roost, so with no argument from Nashville, they were settled!

The wedding was fabulous. Twy, beautifully attired, sauntered down the aisle playing her fiddle, to the waiting Groom, strumming the bouzouki. It was clear they make beautiful music together! The knot was lovingly tied, while the chickens respectfully waited until after the ceremony to cluck and crow, loudly and clearly! Both chickens volunteered for the clean-up committee and disposed of all the table scraps, feeling honored to partake in the Wedding Banquet. The day was a great success! Twy and John were officially, and in every sense of the word, "Entwyned'!

Sunday was relaxed and joyous. Thanks to Nashville, no one overslept, and the morning was brimming with coffee and music. "Amazing Grace, how sweet the sound" ...and the chickens "sang" along. The day was fine and we spent much of the afternoon basking in the sun out on the wrap-around porch. Nashville and Nugget hunted and pecked contentedly while we chatted, nibbled and played music, with Nashville crowing along every now and again.

Soon it was time to get to our Coyote Cowgirl Show on the road; The Cabin was down the road just a few miles. With all the instruments, microphones, musicians and guests, we needed several vehicles. All my equipment was still in the truck, except the guitar, which I had used to sing a wedding song for Twy and John. So, I stowed the guitar in the back of my truck and away we all went. I don't think The Cabin will ever be the same again! We picked and sang, and whooped and howled until every song was sung. The following morning we would be heading home, so finally back to the house we went.

Nashville, again, provided us with prompting for an early departure! Coffee and breakfast treats awaited, and a few more rounds of song. We then loaded our belongings into our vehicles for the respective trips home, and gathered together to say good-bye. I was very much hoping that the loading of the feathered fowl would not seriously delay MY departure. But I need not have worried. In response to last night's foray out to The Cabin, Nashville and Nugget, not wanting be left behind, wasted no time at all loading up once they saw the guitar loaded in!

By the end of our final farewells, Nugget, bless her soul, was already in the travel cage. Nashville, hovering about just outside the door of their vacation home, needed only a gentle reminder that we were, in fact, moving out. The cage door closing on his tail feathers hastened his entry. Then, with the Click! of the latch, and a hearty crow from Nashville, we said "Good-Bye and God-Bless" to Bloomington Indiana, and headed back home to Amazing Grace.

PREDATORS

When living in the country raising chickens, sheep, goats and horses - or even garden plants, one inevitably will have several memorable encounters with Predators!

I have had to reckon with these dramatic moments in my own way.

Every creature has something else that wants to eat it. That is just the way it is! I have come to some sort of peace with it and have tried to gain an understanding of all living things.

Here are two stories that might help you do the same.

MISS MINK

SQUAAAAAAAWK !! SQUAAAAAAAAAWK!! I was unpleasantly jolted from a gentle slumber early one March morning, at barely first light. I knew that sound! Something was attacking my hens! In a moment, I was outside and running toward the barn before I was even awake enough to think. The brisk morning air quickly brought me to my senses. I was halfway there, but without my contact lenses, coat or boots. I was barefoot, in fact. "So what?" I thought, "How long will it take me to scare away whatever is out there terrorizing my hens?"

The ground was frozen, with a thick frost on it, but by noon it would likely be warming. I kept going... frightened for my flock. I looked around, squinting, wondering where I had left the shovel

I'd used in the garden the day before. I could maybe ward off the offending predator with the darn thing! Or, at the very least, protect myself with it.

It's a little crazy-scary going out into near dark to face a wild animal, especially not knowing what it is. A fox? A pack of raccoons? A sneaky little weasel, a hungry coyote or what? Some deeply heroic part of yourself kicks in when something you love and are bound to protect is in danger.

You transform into a brave warrior! I had faced many predators before, at one time or another, but never from such a vulnerable position. That morning I was barefoot and blind, plunging into near-darkness to defend my hens. Straight to the coop I ran, still glancing around for the shovel, only to realize that the ruckus and the danger were elsewhere. All was still as stone behind the henhouse door. But! From the horse-training pen between the cabin and the pasture right next door, came again the dreadful commotion.

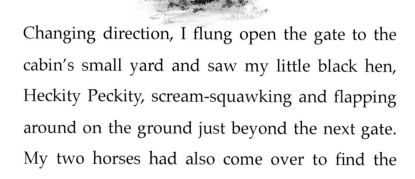

Changing direction, I flung open the gate to the cabin's small yard and saw my little black hen, Heckity Peckity, scream-squawking and flapping around on the ground just beyond the next gate. My two horses had also come over to find the cause of the disturbance, and both were standing on the other side of the training pen, bending their heads down over the fence close to the hen.

The evening before had been the first warmish night in early Spring, a notorious time for predators. Unbeknownst to me, my independent-minded black hen, Heckity-Peckity, had been reluctant to go back to roost in the henhouse.

The poultry had been cooped up all winter, so she had opted for camping out that night. The previous night, at Birdy-Bedtime when I tuck them all in, I had noticed that she was missing. I searched around the farmyard in the failing light, but could not find her. Assuming the worst, I had sadly and reluctantly closed the henhouse door without her.

Now, here she was, screaming hysterically for help! In time for me, but not so for my hen, I saw the cause of her distress. A wildly determined little Mink was dancing all around her, bobbing and weaving, and baring its razor-sharp teeth, making a sort of hissing noise and squaring off with both the horses and me. Undaunted, I ran up to the gate, shooing and shouting and waving my hands, making every attempt to frighten the wild thing away.

But this fierce little creature, less than two feet long, stood her ground, unquestionably ready to defend her meal! There was just no way I could get any closer without boots or shovel!

In a frustrated panic, I ran back to the house to equip myself properly. But, just as I had dreaded, by the time I returned prepared for battle, it was too late. The mink had already killed Heckity-Peckity and dragged her part way under the barn for the feast. I just stood there, horrified and heartbroken, and cried! I was so sad and upset with myself. If only I had been braver! And why hadn't I just put on my stupid boots before leaving the house?!

But now, of course, there was nothing I could do. I leaned on the fence in the cool of the morning to watch the sun rise, trying to calm down.

The birds began their morning choir. Bright and beautiful rose the sun, into a brilliant blue sky. I began to feel more at peace.

"I will surely miss my Little Heckity Peckity," I mused wistfully. She had been such a friendly hen. And a good little egg-layer, too. We had named her from the nursery rhyme –

Heckity Peckity my black Hen
She lays eggs for gentlemen
Sometimes nine and sometimes ten!
Heckity-Peckity, my black Hen.

This is a silly rhyme, as hens can only lay one egg per day...two at the very most! What hens will do, however, if living in one house together, is lay all their eggs in one "Broody Box". These are boxes built into the henhouse where hens lay their eggs, and will occasionally "set" long enough to hatch a brood. A setting hen is also called a "broody hen", and thus the name "Broody Box". If a child went out collecting the eggs, and saw but one hen in the box with so many eggs, it is likely the child might credit the sitting hen with all the eggs in the box. But, actually, each hen has her own special color and sized egg that she lays. When you have a small flock, you come to know which hen lays which egg!. Heckity-Peckity was a Cochin with hilarious feathery feet. Because she was a Bantam, she was also very small, as were her pure white eggs.

She was the only Bantam in the barnyard, and I always used her eggs whenever I was halving a recipe. The bantam egg is so small it's like only half an egg! I loved finding her little white egg among the large brown, blue and speckled eggs of the larger birds. Oh! and she was so friendly! So small and so cute. And she would always let me pick her up and stroke her. She had been a very special girl.

"Yes, little Heckity-Peckity, I will truly miss you," I smiled at the thought of her.

"Ah, but the little Mink," I thought at last. "Surely at least She is happy. She must have been very, very hungry to have stood her ground against three such enormous creatures as the horses and me! What a brave girl! And she looks so much like my ferret, only... wearing a mink coat! " My heart warmed a bit toward this little creature. It was very rare to see a mink where I live, I had only seen one other in all my years, and I really wanted to get a closer look! And I absolutely needed to catch and remove the offending hen-slayer anyway, before she decimated my flock. I made a decision .

I took the dead little hen and put her in my "Have-A-Heart" trap. It is designed to catch animals alive. I left the trap where I had found the dead hen. I knew Miss Mink would be coming back for more chicken! And, sure enough, within two hours she was in the trap with the hen!

The day was indeed warming, so I brought out some water in a dispenser designed for guinea pigs, gerbils and such. I threw a towel over the cage, and moved it carefully into the barn, out of the sun. I gave the little mink the water which she gratefully drank, keeping her eye on me all the while. I came to visit her several times during that day, bringing her water and treats of dry cat food crunchies.

By evening the barn had a very strong odor...Peee -U! It smelled like skunk! That little Mink sure knew how to stink! It made me wonder how on earth anyone could come to the conclusion that it was a good idea to make coats from the fur of these small, smelly creatures! She smelled awful! But that is because mink, especially when they are searching for a mate, exude a pungent musk...a sort of built in perfume! It is stinky to us, but other mink love it!! Hmmmmmmmmm... I had another idea. Being Spring, it was very likely that this little girl mink had a boyfriend! Maybe I could catch him as well, while I had such tasty bait.

I got out an old cat-carrying case, filled it with fresh hay and allowed my captive mink to release into it. I then put the live trap, tunnel style, directly in front of Miss Mink's new home. I figured either the female mink or the tasty chicken would lure the boyfriend, if there was one, into the trap! But the next morning, there was no new mink to be found. I still wasn't taking chances, so I kept the arrangement intact for a while longer. Each day I would take water and a couple cat crunchies out to Miss Mink. She was still able to reach the chicken, so she was living well! Each day she became more and more accustomed to me. She didn't back away when I approached, even when I put the offerings into her cage... In fact, she seemed to like my company!! By the third day she would come right out of her hay bed to greet me. I would feed her then, and we would just hang out together, enjoying each other for a while.

After the fifth day, I had still not trapped another mink. She must have just been passing through when I caught her. She was young, so perhaps she had just left home. But MY farm would not be a suitable place for a mink to take up residence. As much as I was enjoying my new friend, I knew it would be best to take her and let her go. Still, when I picked up her cage to load her on the truck, she neither cowered nor attacked. She seemed completely at ease. She seemed so sweet, part of me just wanted to keep her for a pet. But, of course, I didn't. A small cage is no place for wildlife to live. And, although she seemed fairly tame, I never did try to pet her. The memory of her sharp teeth and fierce attitude kept me very respectful of this little creature. Chickens and mink are a bad mix, and besides, mink are really stinky! She stunk up the whole barn!

I drove her to a large tract of State Land several miles from my house. Knowing how mink love water, I found a shady spot down by a gently flowing stream. There, I let her, and what was left of Heckity-Peckity, go. I could leave knowing Miss Mink would have something to eat while she adjusted to her new surroundings. It had been very difficult to lose my sweet black hen to the mink, very sad, indeed. But, I discovered that although I had lost one friend, I had gained another. Now...it was time to say good-bye to both.

A Promise Kept

For over a week, chickens had been disappearing from the barnyard. Back then I had over twenty-five birds in the coop. This was back in the early days of my hen-raising career, and all of these gals had been ordered from the Murray McMurry Chicken Catalogue and hand-raised in large part by my children. So, of course, they all had names ...silly and precious names like Peepster, Top Hat and Molasses.

It was early summer and the days were long and lovely. One afternoon, the children and I went visiting some friends. The evening came on so gentle and warm that we ended up staying much longer than planned. It was well after dark before we came back, so tired we went straight to bed. We had had a wonderful time, but...Oh! No! We had all forgotten to close the henhouse door! Next morning, when we went out to feed them, we found four of our dear hens were missing. We all felt horrible, but especially me. I was the adult and the wellbeing of the hens was ultimately my responsibility. I would have to be more diligent! After that night, I began taking extra precautions to close them in every evening, right at sunset.

But, then, the hens began to disappear at random times during the day. It was the signature trademark of the Fox! I started staying outside with them as much as possible in the daytime, occupying myself with weeding and planting, hanging out laundry, and outdoor tasks of all sorts. But the damage was done, and I could not be outside every minute. By now, thirteen hens were missing.

I knew that this fox must either have a family, or had opened up a chicken stand somewhere in the neighborhood.

As it turns out, my friends just down the street had discovered a fox den on their property. They had even been fortunate enough to see the little kits with their Momma! I too love foxes and hoped to see the kits, but I didn't want my hens providing their baby food! I was determined that the fox's chicken-thieving days would soon be coming to an abrupt

In early summer, both the sun and I are always up early. So, at first light, I had been out to feed the horses and what was left of my flock. That morning, the hens were clearly nervous, pecking absently at their cracked corn and peering about, sticking close by me. I talked to them reassuringly and promised I would keep them safe.

Now, being a farmer, I had a gun to protect my animals here on the farm. And I decided that if ever there was one, this was the appropriate time to use it. One or two hens missing I may have been able to forgive, but not thirteen! That was too many! My poor little flock was traumatized and at this rate I would soon be altogether out of hensI

I came inside and stood there gazing out the window, washing up some dishes and wondering what to do. Some movement across the meadow caught my eye!

"What's this? Could it be...?" YES! Out from the woods and into the field The Fox strode boldly forth! He must have been watching me perform my morning ritual: I would go first thing to the barn to feed the horses and chickens, letting the hens out of their coop. Then I would return to the house for breakfast and house chores. Now, he figured, he was safe to make his raid! Clever fox!

He had slyly come in from the opposite direction of his den, so he must have circled up and around my house. Oh! He WAS clever!

And he was handsome! A husky Red Fox with a fine and bushy tail! I stopped everything and stared, the soap bubbles still dancing on my hands. In his fine and foxlike manner he trotted directly towards the hen-pen. He meant business! I imagined him reviewing his grocery list and contemplating his morning meal.

I grabbed the gun.

Slipping out the back door, I was determined to take him by surprise. My bare feet were silent in the warm, wet grass. So intent was he on his prey that he did not see me until I had him in my sights, trigger cocked.

He was but three yards from the hens, with only the wire fence in between them, when he felt my eyes upon him. He looked directly at me, and our eyes locked. I was furious at him for stealing all my hens, but I must say, he was very handsome indeed, and I considered his family. I could not help but admire him and wish him a different fate.

AND! At that same and very moment came "a Voice"... not from out-side me, but from somewhere IN-side me, as loud and distinct as hearing with my ears. From where it came, God only knows.

"He only wants what you want!" said The Voice, plain and clear. I knew, instantly... this was The Truth.

"Oh! I know that! I know that!" came the cry from in my heart. "I know he has a family to feed. But I can't let him keep killing my chickens! NO! I love them and I am sworn to protect them!"

The fox stood there, staring, eyes locked with mine for a few eternal seconds, while I contemplated his fate. Into my heart flooded compassion and resolve...and through my eyes I said to that Fox, "FOX! I'm going to give you This One Chance!

Today, I will not pull this trigger! BUT! If I ever, if I ever catch you here again, I WILL."

IMMEDIATELY he turned and beat a hasty retreat. He knew I meant business! He was getting out while the getting was good!

To my eternal amazement and gratitude, The Fox never took, not even one, more of my hens that Spring. Or that Summer. Or that Fall. In fact, I had no hen loss due to foxes for several years. My neighbors down the street, who also had hens, were not as fortunate. But I feel sure that they had not offered the Fox the same options.

 Over the course of those several years, I did see that Fox again, three separate times, once walking, but twice just sitting...near the apple tree, across the road from my Farm.

He was not standing. He was sitting, looking over at the forbidden territory, toward the hens. But the last time that I saw him there, he was old and thin, his fur mangy and matted. He may have even been hungry. But he just sat there. He was an Old Fox now, and I knew that soon he would surely die. He had lived a good long life. Whatever all else he may have done, he had earned his Grace from me and relieved my Spirit of both guilt and regret. The Fox and I were at peace. We had both kept our promise.

AFTERWORD

I hope you have enjoyed reading these stories as much as I've enjoyed sharing them. I hope they've brought you new understanding and appreciation for the animals in your life. I am always amazed at the intelligence and sensitivity certain animals possess and how each one is so unique. Maybe you have already had some astonishing or deeply moving experiences with your own pets or creatures from the wild.

Perhaps you will get the chance to visit Amazing Grace Bed and Breakfast, here in beautiful Upstate New York, and swap some Animal Magic stories with me. I know I would enjoy hearing them. And I hope I get the opportunity to write more stories, there are so many to tell!

I love animals and I'm sure you do too. Their courage and devotion have changed the course of human history, just as their affection for us changes our hearts. I wish you many special adventures with the animals in your life.

- Alicia Love

29136603R00048

Made in the USA
San Bernardino, CA
15 January 2016